GALAXY ZACK

A GALACTIC EASTER!

By Ray O'Ryan
Illustrated by Colin Jack

LITTLE SIMON
New York London Toronto Sy

LITTLE SIMON
An imprint of Simon & Schuster Children's Publishing Division
1230 Avenue of the Americas, New York, New York 10020

For information about special discounts for bulk purchases, please contact Simon & Schuster Special Sales at 1-866-506-1949 or business@simonandschuster.com.
The Simon & Schuster Speakers Bureau can bring authors to your live event. For more information or to book an event contact the Simon & Schuster Speakers Bureau at 1-866-248-3049 or visit our website at www.simonspeakers.com.
Initial interior design sketches by Andrew Murray
Designed by Nicholas Sciacca
Manufactured in the United States of America 0216 MTN
3 4 5 6 7 8 9 10
Library of Congress Cataloging-in-Publication Data
O'Ryan, Ray.
A galactic Easter! / by Ray O'Ryan ; illustrated by Colin Jack.
pages cm. — (Galaxy Zack ; 7)
Summary: Zack and Drake venture to Gluco, the candy planet, for some Easter fun. But while competing in such activities as an egg toss and a three-legged race, Zack is so determined to come in first that he considers cheating to win.
ISBN 978-1-4424-9357-5 (pbk : alk. paper) — ISBN 978-1-4424-9358-2 (hc : alk. paper) — ISBN 978-1-4424-9359-9 (ebook) [1. Science fiction. 2. Competition (Psychology)—Fiction. 3. Easter—Fiction. 4. Outer space—Fiction.] I. Jack, Colin, illustrator. II. Title.
PZ7.O7843Gal 2014
[Fic]—dc23
2013006952

CONTENTS

Chapter 1	Eggs and Bags	1
Chapter 2	Candy Planet	9
Chapter 3	The Big Day	19
Chapter 4	Welcome to Gluco!	31
Chapter 5	Off to the Races	45
Chapter 6	Let the Games Begin!	57
Chapter 7	Find the Eggs	69
Chapter 8	The Race Is On!	83
Chapter 9	Zack's Decision	99
Chapter 10	A Very Happy Easter!	109

Chapter 1

Eggs and Bags

Zack Nelson stared into his hyper-phone. On the screen he saw Bert, his best friend from Earth. Zack and his family used to live on Earth. Now they lived on the planet Nebulon.

"What are you doing today, Bert?" asked Zack.

"We're painting Easter eggs," Bert replied.

In the background Zack could see Roberta and Darlene, Bert's two younger sisters. The girls ran into the room carrying a painting set and a basket full of eggs.

"Remember when we used to decorate eggs together?" Zack asked.

"That was pretty cool," said Bert. "Remember doing the egg toss?"

"Totally!" replied Zack. "Especially the year I missed the catch and the egg landed on my new shoes!"

"And what about the sack races?"

"Oh, they were funny. Hop, hop, hop . . . fall! Hop, hop, hop . . . fall!"

Zack and Bert both started laughing hysterically.

"So how do they celebrate Easter there on Nebulon?" asked Bert.

Zack thought for a moment.

"You know, Bert, I'm not really sure," he replied. "This is our first Easter here."

"Are there eggs on Nebulon?" Bert asked.

"I know there aren't any chickens here," Zack explained. "When we eat eggs, they're the eggs of the rondo bird. And those eggs are big and round like softballs."

"Excuse me, Master Just Zack," said a voice from a speaker just above Zack.

"What's up, Ira?" Zack asked.

Ira was the Nelson family's Indoor Robotic Assistant. Although he was a machine, Ira had quickly become a part of the Nelson family.

"Dinner will be ready in five minutes," Ira explained.

"Thanks, Ira. I'll be right down," said Zack. "Gotta go, Bert. Happy Easter! Let's vid-chat again soon."

"See ya, Zack."

How will we celebrate Easter? Zack wondered as he left his room and headed downstairs for dinner.

Chapter 2
Candy Planet

Zack arrived at the kitchen table. The booth hovered above the floor. Beside him sat his older twin sisters, Cathy and Charlotte. On the other side sat his mom and dad, Shelly and Otto.

"Dinner is served," said Ira.

A panel in the wall slid open. A

mechanical arm served steaming plates of food.

"Thank you, Ira," said Mom. "All of this looks delicious!"

"So, Dad . . . ," Cathy began.

". . . what are we doing . . . ," Charlotte added.

". . . for Easter this year?" Cathy concluded.

The twins often finished each other's sentences or spoke as if they were one person.

Dad had a mouthful of food. Before he could reply, the girls continued.

"Will we get to . . ."

". . . decorate eggs or go on an Easter egg hunt?"

"What about chocolate bunnies . . ."

". . . with tiny treats and surprises hidden inside?"

Dad swallowed his food.

"Great news, everyone," he said. "We are going to the planet Gluco for Easter!"

"No way!" Zack shouted excitedly. "The Candy Planet! That is so grape!"

"The Candy Planet?" the twins asked together.

"Why do you . . ."

". . . call it that, Zack?"

"Are you kidding?" said Zack. "Just about everything on Gluco is made out of candy! I can't imagine a cooler place to spend Easter!"

"Not only that, guys," said Dad, "but they also have an Easter race course with sack races and other contests."

"Yay!" cried Zack.

"And they have an egg decorating workshop with colors you didn't even know existed!" Dad explained.

"Okay . . ."

". . . let's go . . ."

". . . to the Candy Planet!"

"Mom, can Drake come with us?" Zack asked.

Drake was Zack's best friend on Nebulon.

"If it's all right with Drake's parents, I don't see why not," replied Mom.

Zack smiled. "This is going to be the best Easter ever!"

After dinner, Zack immediately got on his hyperphone with Drake.

"I love going to Gluco!" Drake exclaimed when Zack told him the plan. "My parents have taken me there lots of times. Let me check with them."

Zack's hyperphone went dark. A few minutes later, Drake's face popped up again.

"My folks said yes!" said Drake excitedly. "What time do we leave?"

"Grape!" cried Zack. "We head to the spaceport at nine on Sunday morning. See you then!"

Imagine. A planet made of candy, Zack thought, just before he drifted off to sleep. *Back when I lived on Earth, I might have made up something like that for a story. But here, it's real!*

Chapter 3
The Big Day

"Time to get up, Master Just Zack," said Ira early Sunday morning.

Zack bolted upright in his bed.

"What day is it, Ira?" he asked, rubbing the sleep from his eyes.

"It is Sunday," Ira replied. "Time to go to Gluco."

Zack jumped from bed and headed downstairs.

"Happy Easter, Zack!" said Mom.

"Happy Easter, everyone!" said Zack.

"Look what . . ."

". . . we got . . ."

". . . for Easter!" said Charlotte and Cathy.

Each girl held up a big chocolate bunny.

"Wow!" exclaimed Zack. "Just like we had on Earth!"

"I ordered them just for the three of you," said Mom. She handed Zack his chocolate bunny.

"Thanks, Mom!" said Zack.

"Excited about today?" asked Mom.

"About going to a planet made of candy?" replied Zack. "Why would I be excited about *that*?"

Zack, his parents, and his sisters all chuckled.

"Cosmic cakes with zoomberry syrup please, Ira," Zack said.

A few seconds later a panel in the kitchen wall slid open and a steaming plate of food came out. Zack poured dark blue syrup all over the flat fluffy cakes shaped like stars and planets.

"Hurry up, Zack . . ."

". . . we have eggs . . ."

". . . to decorate on Gluco!" said Charlotte and Cathy.

"Mrph . . . mpfruf," replied Zack through a mouthful of cosmic cakes.

"Master Drake has arrived," Ira announced.

Drake strolled into the room.

"Good morning, everyone," Drake said. "Thank you for inviting me on this trip."

"We're glad you could make it," replied Mom.

"Okay—I'm ready!" Zack said, tossing his napkin onto his empty plate and jumping from his seat. "Let's go!"

"What about . . ."

". . . Luna?"

"Can she come?" asked the twins.

"It wouldn't be a family trip without Luna!" said Dad. "Come on, girl!"

Everyone piled into the family's flying car and headed to the Creston City Spaceport. A short while later they climbed into a shuttle and took off.

Zack smiled as stars and planets whizzed past him. Space travel always made him happy. Zack and Drake played games on their hyperphones until . . .

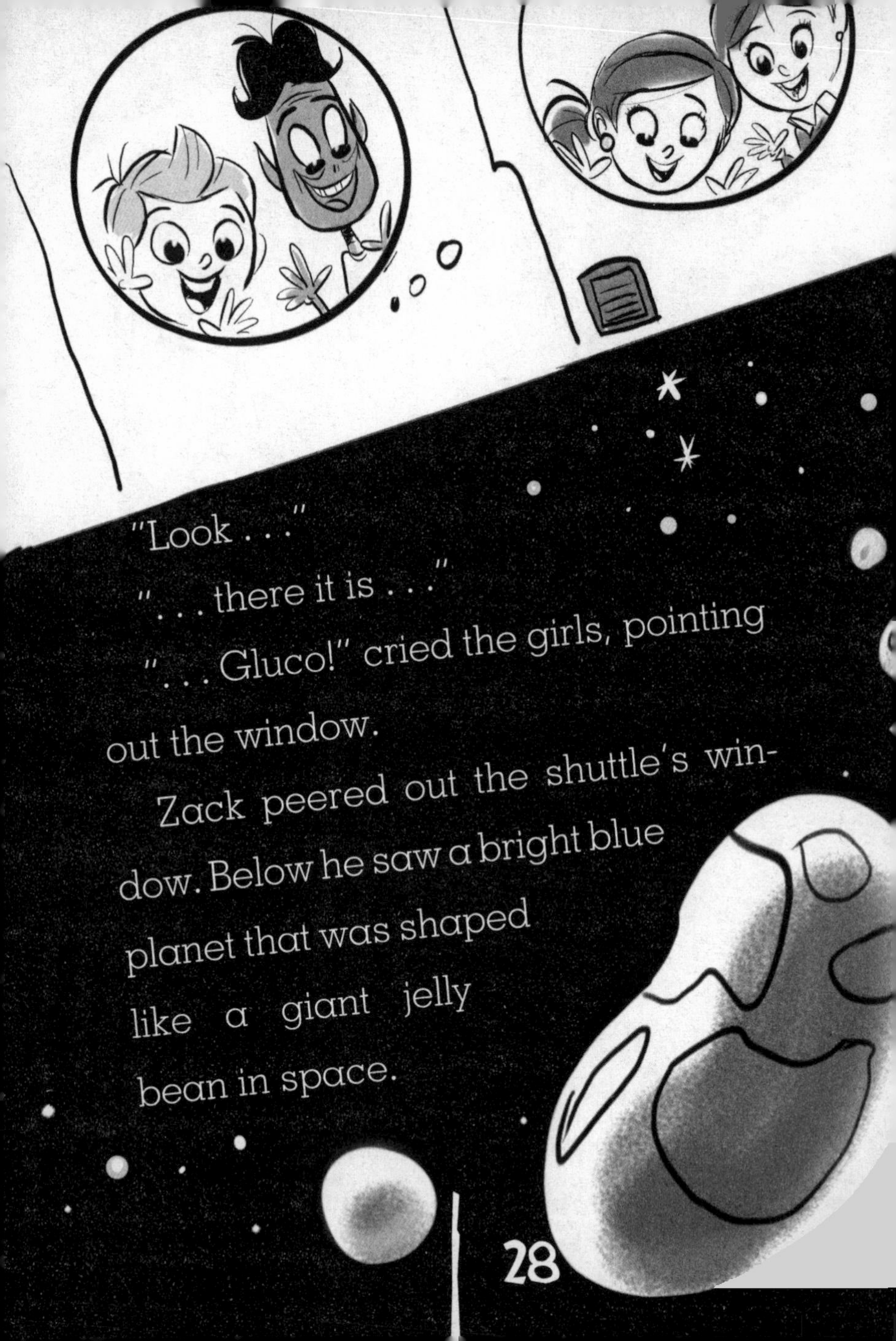

"Look . . ."

". . . there it is . . ."

". . . Gluco!" cried the girls, pointing out the window.

Zack peered out the shuttle's window. Below he saw a bright blue planet that was shaped like a giant jelly bean in space.

As the shuttle dropped down for its landing, it passed through what looked like a layer of clouds.

"These clouds are made of cotton candy!" said Drake.

"This is going to be great!" cried Zack.

Chapter 4
Welcome to Gluco!

Charlotte and Cathy stared out the window of a space bus.

"Look at . . ."

". . . all the . . ."

". . . colors!" they squealed.

The bus carried them from the Gluco spaceport into the center of

the largest city on the planet, Caramel City.

Rivers of golden caramel snaked through the streets.

"Look at that bridge!" cried Zack, pointing out the window. "I think it's made out of peppermint sticks!"

"And there is a garden

filled with lollipop sunflower plants," said Drake.

"Look at that tree!" Zack shouted. "The bark looks like it's made from licorice."

"It is," explained Drake. "And those white fluffy flowers? They are marshmallows."

"Amazing!" said Mom.

"Delicious!" added Dad.

"Those houses look like they are made of gingerbread," said Zack.

"They are," said Drake.

The bus pulled up to a huge building shaped like a giant Easter egg.

"First stop, the egg decorating workshop," announced the driver.

The Nelsons and Drake got off the bus and walked into the silver building. Luna sniffed everything in sight.

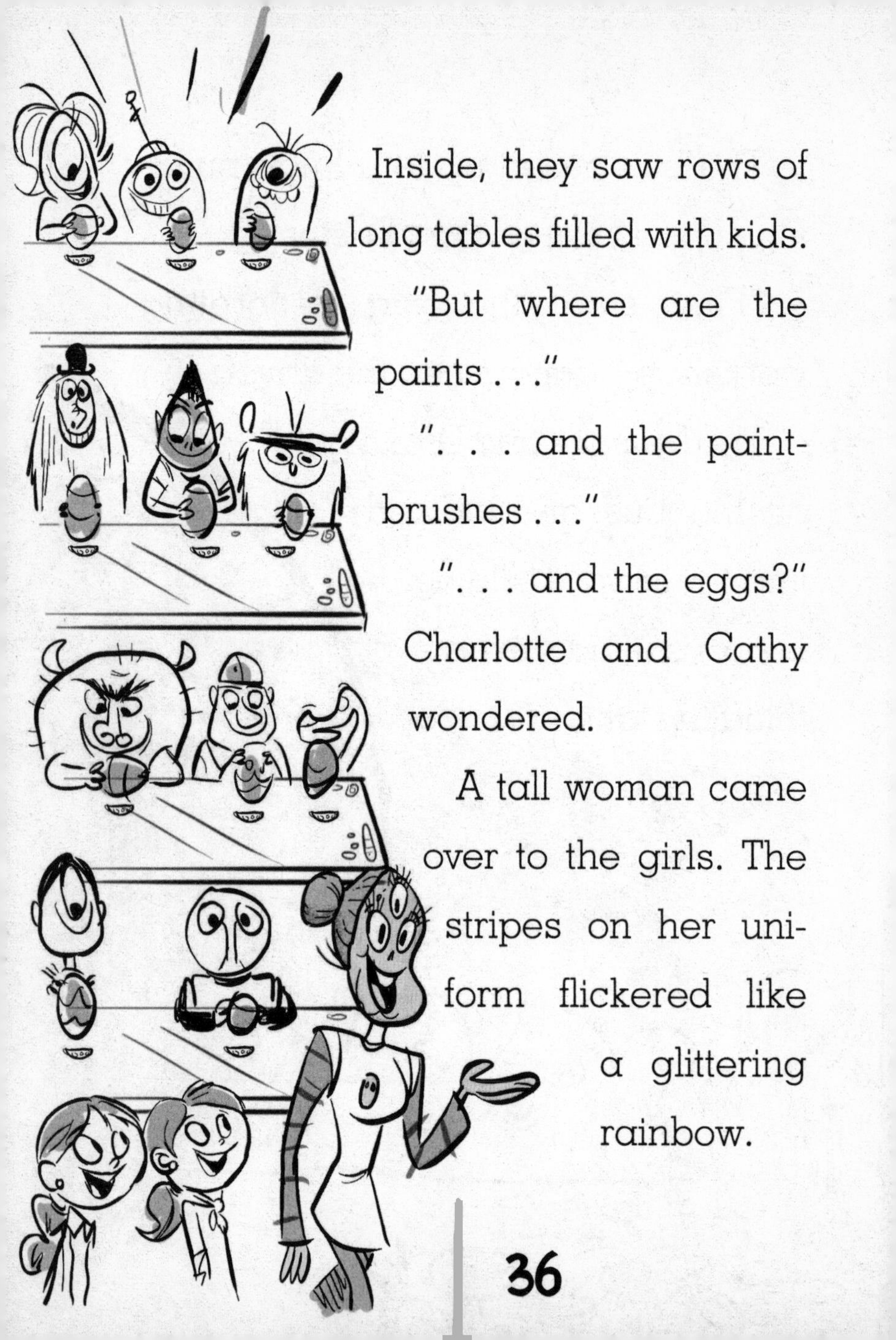

Inside, they saw rows of long tables filled with kids.

"But where are the paints . . ."

". . . and the paint-brushes . . ."

". . . and the eggs?" Charlotte and Cathy wondered.

A tall woman came over to the girls. The stripes on her uni-form flickered like a glittering rainbow.

"You must be new to Gluco," said the woman. "I am Cigney. Let me show you how we decorate eggs."

Cigney led Charlotte and Cathy to one of the long tables. In front of each girl sat a small, egg-shaped machine.

"Start by touching the egg in front of you," explained Cigney.

When Cathy touched the machine, it began to glow.

"Now use your fingers as if they were paint brushes," said Cigney. "As you paint with your fingers, call out colors."

Cathy began to trace a swirling pattern on the egg-shaped machine. "Red!" she called out. Wherever she moved her finger, a swirl of red appeared on the machine.

"Green!" called out Charlotte. She drew criss-crossing patterns of green onto her machine.

"Blue!" said Cathy, adding blue streaks to her design.

When Charlotte's entire machine was covered in colors, Cigney said, "Now press the button on the top of the machine."

Charlotte pressed the button. A panel on the machine opened and out came a colorful Easter egg. The egg was decorated exactly in the pattern Charlotte had traced.

"Wow . . ."

". . . this is . . ."

". . . amazing!"

"Would you like to paint another egg?" Cigney asked.

"Sure!" both girls shouted at once.

"I'll stay here with the girls," said Dad. "Shelly, why don't you take Zack

and Drake to the race course for the games?"

"Okay," said Mom. "Let's go."

"*Now* you're talking!" said Zack.

Chapter 5
Off to the Races

Zack, Mom, and Drake hurried from the egg decorating workshop. Luna followed them. On the way to the race course, they passed some amazing-looking trees.

"That's one of those licorice trees!" exclaimed Zack. "Is it really licorice?"

"Go ahead and try some," replied Drake.

Zack peeled off a tiny piece of the tree's bark. He slowly took a bite.

"Mmmmm," he moaned. "It really is!"

Then Zack plucked off one of the fluffy white flowers

growing in the grass. "Marshmallow! It really *is* a marshmallow!" he said as the gooey, sticky treat melted in his mouth."

Luna rolled around in the marsh-mallow flowers. When she got up she was covered with marshmallows. She spun around in circles trying to lick the white puffs off of her fur.

"Silly girl," said Zack, plucking off a few marshmallows.

"Hey, Zack—look at this!" cried Drake. He knelt down next to a colorful bush. Dangling from the plant's many green stems were jelly beans of every color. He popped one into his mouth. "Yum! Watermelon flavored."

"Let's try this," Zack suggested. He pulled two pink petals from a flower on a nearby vine and handed one to Drake.

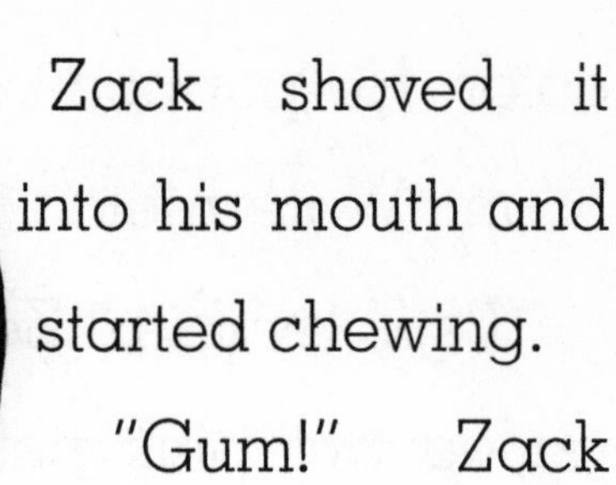

Zack shoved it into his mouth and started chewing.

"Gum!" Zack cried. "It's bubble gum!"

Zack picked a few more gum petals and slipped them into his pocket. The boys chewed on the gum and blew bubbles as they continued to the race course. A few minutes later they arrived at a big field.

"You boys sign up," said Mom. "I'm going to go see how the twins are doing. I'll be back soon. Come on, Luna!"

As Luna walked away, she jumped up onto a tree and bit off a long piece of licorice. She happily chewed on the candy as she followed Mom.

"Hello, boys," said a man at the sign-up table. "My name is Larso.

Which activities would you like to compete in?"

"All of them!" replied Zack. He recalled how much he loved every Easter event back on Earth.

"Okay, just put your names here," said Larso. "We have two people on each team. I assume you guys want to be a team?"

"You bet!" exclaimed Zack.

"Thank you," added Drake.

"Each two-person team is matched up against another two-person team for the events," explained Larso.

"Sounds great!" said Zack. "Who are we competing against?"

"Here they come now," said Larso, pointing to two boys who were walking toward Zack and Drake.

"It's Seth Stevens from Sprockets Academy," said Zack. Zack and Seth hadn't gotten along at first, but over time they had become friendlier.

"And he is with his best friend, Howie!" Drake said.

"Drake," Zack said very seriously. "I like Seth and Howie, but I really want to win this contest!"

Chapter 6

Let the Games Begin!

"All contestants for the egg tossing contest please line up!" Larso announced into a bullhorn.

"That's the first event," Zack said. He and Drake headed to the starting line.

Zack and Drake faced each other.

They stood about a foot apart. Nearby, Seth and Howie lined up in the same position.

"I am really good at this event, Zack," said Seth.

"Me too," replied Zack.

"May the best team win," said Drake.

"Do not worry," said Howie. "We will!"

"Here are the

rules," said Larso. "One player tosses an egg to his partner who must catch the egg without breaking it. After each successful catch, the teammates will take a step away from each other. The first team to drop or break the egg loses."

Larso handed

Zack a colorfully decorated egg. Then he handed one to Seth.

"Ready?" Larso announced in a booming voice. "Begin!"

Zack tossed his egg into the air with a gentle underhand motion. The egg rose, then dropped into Drake's cupped hands. It remained unbroken.

Seth went next. He lobbed his egg softly. It arced through the air and landed in Howie's outstretched hand.

"Step!" called out Larso.

Zack and Drake each took one step backward. So did Seth and Howie.

Now it was Drake's turn. He reached his arm out and released the egg, all in one smooth motion. The egg floated through the air. Zack cupped his hands and caught the egg, pulling his arms toward his body. The egg remained unbroken.

Howie sent an underhand toss sailing toward Seth. Seth's eyes opened wide as he realized that Howie had thrown the egg a bit too hard. Seth stepped backward, reached up, and plucked the egg out of the air with one hand. The egg was intact.

"Step!" Larso shouted again.

Both sets of teammates took another step apart.

Zack concentrated hard. Drake looked very far away. Zack tossed the egg high into the air—higher than any of his previous throws.

Drake took a step to his

left and reached his hands out. As the egg came down, he brought his hands together—but not fast enough. The egg slipped through Drake's hands and hit the ground. The shell cracked, and purple sugary powder from inside puffed up into the air.

Larso blew a whistle. "The egg

toss goes to Seth and Howie," he announced.

"Sorry about that throw," said Zack as he and Drake headed over to the next event.

"No problem," replied Drake.

"Let's win the next event," Zack said to Drake.

"That is the plan," Drake replied.

Chapter 7
Find the Eggs

The boys arrived at a large open field filled with tall boxes, tubes, and a maze. Large holes in the ground led to tunnels.

"The next event is the Easter egg hunt," Larso announced. "The eggs are made of metal. You will use these

findex devices to locate as many eggs as you can in five minutes."

Larso then handed out a thin silver stick and a sack to each of the four boys.

Zack pressed a button on the stick and a tiny antenna popped out of the tip and started spinning.

"Ready?" shouted Larso. "Begin!"

Zack ran toward a tall wooden box. A red laser shot from his findex. The thin beam bounced off the box and disappeared down a nearby hole in the ground.

"I think I got one!" Zack yelled. He climbed down into the hole and found himself in an underground tunnel. The red laser light from his findex vanished. In its place, a flashlight beam lit his way.

Just ahead, Zack spotted three small shelves jutting out from the side of

the tunnel. On each shelf sat a colorful metal egg. Zack snatched up the three eggs and placed them into the sack that hung from his shoulder.

When he came out of the tunnel, Zack spotted Drake stepping out from a long plastic tube.

"I got two!" Drake shouted, holding up his sack.

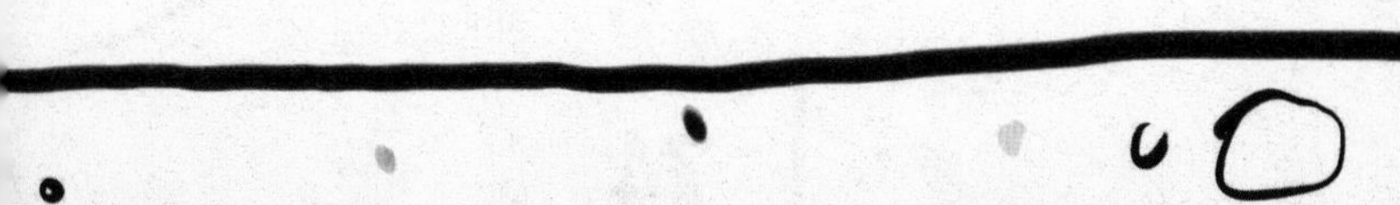

"Three!" Zack yelled back.

Zack's findex started spinning again. A red laser bounced off a nearby tree and vanished into a maze. The maze was made from a series of shaped bushes that twisted and turned.

Zack hurried into the maze's entrance. After he walked a short distance, one path split off to the right.

Should I turn or go straight? Zack wondered. *I need to find more eggs, but I don't want to get lost in here.*

He held his findex above his head. The red laser shot off to the right.

Right it is!

Moving quickly, Zack made his way down the twisting path. Up ahead he spotted something resting on top of the maze's wall.

"Another egg!" Zack cried. He snatched the painted egg from the top of the wall.

By the time Zack reached the end of the maze he had collected four more Easter eggs.

Zack stepped out of the maze. He spotted Drake climbing down a tall ladder. Zack held up his sack.

"Four more!" he shouted.

"Two more!" Drake replied.

"The Easter egg hunt is now over," Larso announced. "The contestants will line up their eggs."

Zack and Drake hurried over to a long table. Seth and Howie stood

on the other side of the table, pulling Easter eggs from their sacks.

When the eggs were all lined up, Larso made an official count.

"Seth and Howie, eleven eggs," said Larso. "Zack and Drake, twelve eggs.

The winners are Zack and Drake."

"High five!" said Zack raising his right hand.

"High huh?" Drake asked. A puzzled look spread across his face.

"It's something we did back on Earth when we won a game or when something really great happened," Zack

explained. "You just slap your right hand against mine over our heads."

Zack raised his hand again. This time Drake reached up and the boys slapped hands.

"High five!" said Drake.

Chapter 8
The Race Is On!

"The next event is the three-legged race," Larso announced.

"I was always great at this back on Earth," Zack whispered to Drake.

Larso handed a black licorice rope to Zack and another rope to Seth. "Each pair of contestants will tie one

of their legs to their partner's. The race will take place over this fifty-yard track. The first pair to cross the finish line is the winner."

Zack and Drake stood side by side. Zack wrapped the candy rope around

his right leg and Drake's left leg, and then he tied it securely. Seth and Howie did the same. The four boys lined up at the starting line.

"Ready?" shouted Larso. "Begin!"

The boys started running. At first Drake and Zack stumbled a bit.

"The trick is to move the legs we have tied together at the same time," Zack explained, "like they're one leg."

Seth and Howie had obviously done this before. They pulled out to an early lead.

But Zack and Drake finally fell into a steady rhythm. They each stepped forward with their outside legs at the same time, then stepped forward with the inside two that were tied together. After a few strides, they had caught up with Seth and Howie.

"Go, Zack!" shouted Dad's voice from the sidelines.

Zack turned and spotted his dad cheering him on. Luna was at his side.

All of a sudden Luna dashed out onto the course. She headed straight for the black licorice ropes tied around Zack's and Drake's legs.

"Luna!" cried Zack. "We're right in the middle of a race!"

But Luna ignored him and grabbed the licorice rope in her teeth and pulled it loose. The licorice tumbled to the ground where Luna happily gobbled it up.

Larso blew a whistle.

"Zack and Drake are disqualified," he said. "Seth and Howie win the three-legged race."

"I'm sorry, Zack," said Dad. He led Luna away. "I'll try to keep Luna on the sidelines."

Zack shook his head.

"Forget it, Zack," said Drake. "We will beat them in the sack race!"

Zack and Drake made their way to the course for the sack race. Only it wasn't a course at all. It was a raised metal platform divided into four sections. A shiny, silvery sack sat on each platform. Each boy stepped into a sack.

A flat screen rested above each platform. Hanging from each screen

was a helmet with high-tech goggles. The goggles blinked with multicolored lights.

"Each contestant hops up and down in place," Larso explained. "In your goggles, you'll see yourself hopping along the course. The faster you hop,

the faster you'll race down the virtual track. Ready? Begin!"

Zack started hopping in place. Although really he was just hopping up and down in the same spot, in his goggles Zack felt like he was speeding down a long race track.

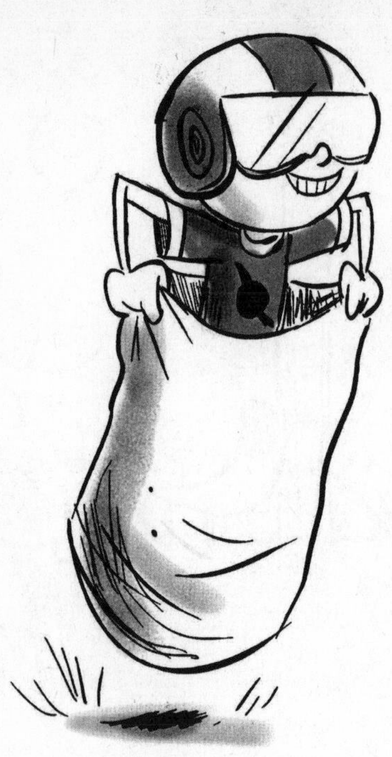

He saw Drake hopping along beside him. He also saw Seth and Howie hopping in the lanes next to them.

This is really fun! Zack thought.

Zack started jumping faster and faster. In his goggles, he saw himself pull away from the other racers. He crossed the finish line well ahead

of everybody else, easily winning the race.

"Yeah!" Zack cried.

"High five!" said Drake, dropping his sack and lifting his hand.

Zack reached up and slapped Drake's hand.

As he stepped down from the platform, Zack spotted his mom. She was standing with Dad and Luna, along with Charlotte and Cathy.

"Great job, Zack!" Mom shouted.

"Go, Zack . . ."

". . . and Drake!" added the twins.

"Contestants, prepare for the final event," announced Larso.

"Each team has won two events," Drake pointed out. "Whoever wins this last one will win the tournament."

"And that is going to be *us*!" said Zack.

Chapter 9
Zack's Decision

"The final event is the egg and spoon contest," Larso explained. "Each contestant must carry an egg on a spoon and pass it onto his teammate's spoon. The team who passes their egg more times in five minutes wins. If either team drops their egg at any time, the

other team wins. Any questions?"

Zack looked at the crowd. He saw his whole family watching, waving, and cheering. The last thing he wanted was to lose in front of all of them.

"We have to win this," Zack whispered to Drake.

"Do not worry, Zack," Drake said. "We will do our best."

"But what if our best is not good enough?" Zack whispered. He looked around to make sure no one could hear him.

"What do you mean?" asked Drake.

Zack pulled a gum petal from his pocket, popped it into his mouth, and started chewing.

"What if I put a tiny piece of bubble gum into the spoon?" he suggested. His voice dropped to an even softer whisper. "Then when I put the egg on the spoon, it will stay put and I can run faster. We'd win for sure!"

Drake's eyes opened wide. He shook his head and looked at Zack in disbelief.

"But—but that would be cheating!" he said. "I do not see the point in winning if we are not the best team, Zack."

"But I really want to win," Zack whined.

"So do I," said Drake, "but winning by cheating is not winning. It is just

cheating. Which is worse than losing."

Zack stepped away from Drake. He needed a moment to be alone and think about all this.

Maybe Drake is right, thought Zack. *After all, how would I feel if I lost and found out that Seth had cheated? I'd be pretty upset. Sure I want to beat Seth, but is it worth it if I don't really beat him?*

"Contestants, report for the egg and spoon contest!" Larso announced.

Zack walked over to Drake.

"You're right, Drake," he said. "Playing fair and having fun is what this is supposed to be about. If we win, we'll win the right way."

Drake smiled and nodded in agreement. "Come on, Zack," he said. "It is time for us to beat them!" he said.

Chapter 10

A Very Happy Easter!

"Ready? Begin!" shouted Larso.

Drake and Zack stood about ten feet apart. Drake started with an egg balanced on his spoon. He walked slowly toward Zack. His eyes never left the egg as he struggled to keep it from tumbling off the spoon.

When he reached Zack, Drake gently rolled the egg onto Zack's spoon.

"Nice!" said Zack. "Now it's my turn."

Drake ran back to his starting spot. Then Zack slowly walked toward him,

carefully balancing the egg.

Zack reached Drake and slipped the egg onto Drake's spoon.

Meanwhile, Seth and Howie were also passing their egg back and forth. Zack glanced at them. It seemed as if Seth and Howie were moving faster.

Come on, Drake, Zack thought as Drake moved toward him. *We have to beat these guys!*

Drake reached Zack and delivered the egg to his spoon once again.

"One minute left!" Larso shouted.

We're running out of time! Zack worried. *Have to hurry*.

"How many times have you guys passed it?" Seth shouted to Zack.

Zack said nothing. He kept his eyes fixed on the egg in his spoon.

Seth couldn't stand it any longer. He had to know how Zack was doing. Seth turned and looked at Zack, taking his eyes off the egg he was carrying. On his next step, Seth's egg tumbled from the spoon and smashed onto the ground.

The game was over. The whole competition was over.

"The final event goes to Zack and Drake," Larso announced. "They win the contest, three games to two!"

Drake and Zack gave each other high fives.

"And here is your prize," said Larso. He handed Zack what looked like a large, colorful Easter egg. It barely fit in the palm of Zack's hand. "Just say what kind of candy you would like and press the button."

"Cotton candy," said Zack, pressing the button on the egg.

The top half of the egg popped open and a cone of cotton candy slid out.

"Yum!" said Zack as he took a bite.

Luna jumped up and also took a big bite out of Zack's cotton candy.

"I guess Luna likes cotton candy too!" said Zack.

He handed the egg to Drake.

"Chocolate bar," said Drake. Again the egg opened. This time a chocolate bar came out.

"You were right, Drake," said Zack as he stuffed more cotton candy into his mouth. "Everything's sweeter when you win the right way."

Zack spotted Seth and Howie at the edge of the field.

"Hey, Seth! Howie!" he called out. "Want some candy?"

Seth slowly took the egg.

"Just say what kind of candy you want and press the button," Zack explained.

"Jelly beans," said Seth. The egg popped open and jelly beans came pouring out into Seth's hand.

"Thanks, Zack," said Seth. "And congratulations on winning."

"Take all you like," Zack said, handing the egg to Howie. "Candy is for everyone!"

"Even . . ."

". . . for . . ."

". . . us?"

Charlotte, Cathy, Mom, and Dad stepped up beside Zack and Drake.

Zack laughed. "Yes, even for you." He handed the egg to Cathy. She asked for licorice. Charlotte asked for lollipops.

"Look at . . ."

". . . the Easter eggs . . ."

". . . we made," the twins said as they gobbled up their candy.

Cathy handed Zack a basket full of beautifully decorated eggs.

"Nice job," said Zack.

"I think everyone had fun today," said Mom.

"You bet!" exclaimed Zack. "I already can't wait to come back to Gluco next Easter!"

CHECK OUT THE NEXT

GALAXY ZACK

ADVENTURE!

HERE'S A SNEAK PEEK!

Nebulon's two suns shone down brightly. It was summer, and the temperature was close to 110 degrees. Zack Nelson and his friend Drake Taylor were trying to figure out what to do to stay cool today.

"We could go back to the indoor

An excerpt from *Drake Makes a Splash!*

snow-slide and ride the slippo-discs down the mondo-hill again," Drake suggested.

"Nah, we did that yesterday," Zack pointed out. "What about going swimming in the Nebu-Dome?"

"I do not think so," replied Drake.

Then Zack spied something up ahead that made his eyes open wide.

"Look!" he said, pointing to a sign in front of the Creston Vivi-Theater. "There's a new vivi-vid playing!"

Vivi-vids were special movies that made people watching them feel like they were part of the movie.

An excerpt from *Drake Makes a Splash!*

"White-Water Wonders!" said Zack, reading the sign. "Putting ourselves into a white-water adventure on a river should cool us right off!"

Zack hurried toward the theater. A few seconds later he realized that Drake was trailing behind him.

"What's wrong, Drake?" he asked. "Don't you think this is a good idea?"

"Well . . ." Drake paused. "Maybe."

"Of course it is!" said Zack. "Come on!"

"Okay, I guess," said Drake.

I wonder what's up with Drake, Zack thought.

An excerpt from *Drake Makes a Splash!*